The
Flowerpot
Bunnies
RETURN

Written by Dr. Carolyn Rehm

Illustrated by Agnes Schanck

Library of Congress Cataloging-in-Publication Data
Rehm, Carolyn, 1952-
Flowerpot Bunnies Return/by Carolyn Rehm

Summary: A true story about the rescue of wild bunnies
and their return to the wild.
1. Bunnies-non-fiction.

ISBN 0-9755390-2-7

Cover and layout designed by Rosemary Carroll and Patti Bishop
All artwork by Agnes Schanck
All photography by Carolyn Rehm
Printed in China
Published by Fith Avenue Press
New York, New York

A portion of the proceeds
from the sale of this book will be donated
by the author to help children with special needs.

I would like to dedicate this book
to the many children who have
touched my life—
my patients, my students,
and my readers!

The winter was long and bitterly cold that year. The mercury often fell below zero, and our snowfall was the heaviest it had been in a long time. Snow piled up high and clung to the delicate branches of the trees and shrubs. It created a magical view that was very different from the lush greens and sparkling rainbow colors of summer.

At first glance, the world seemed dormant as many animals hibernated and others sought the gentle warmth of the South. Yet against this frosty white backdrop in our yard, I spied an occasional wild brown bunny. Hopping about in the snow, it left paw prints as a reminder that life continued in this crystal wonderland.

I often wondered about the "Flowerpot Bunnies" during the long months from December through March. I had rescued the five baby bunnies from their unsafe flowerpot nest the previous summer. After caring for them for several weeks, I had released them back into the wild where they had reunited with their mother.

The bunny mom and her five offspring, namely, Rose, Daisy, Marigold, Dandelion and Cracker Jack, had made our yard their home since that time. But where were they now?

I knew that during the frigid months of winter, rabbits survive by lying in forms, or holes, in the earth. They feed on bark and roots instead of clover and flowers. I worried about the Flowerpot Bunnies and the hardships of cold and frost they had to endure.

Winter gradually faded away and ushered in another spring. This was a time of new beginnings – bright blossoms, fresh clover, and cheerful song burst forth on the awakening world.

One clear morning in April, I was astonished when five lively bunnies appeared together in my backyard. They were the Flowerpot Bunnies all grown up! They put on an amazing show for me as they hopped and played in the emerald grass.

Cracker Jack was still the biggest and he hopped so high that he seemed to soar through the air! I sat on the steps of the deck and spoke to each of them one by one as they hopped in my direction.

"Where is your mother?" I asked with a smile.

They paused to listen and then continued their lively game of tag.

Later that same week the bunny mom suddenly showed up on my back deck! When I discovered her there, I stopped and stared. She looked older and thinner. I noticed with surprise that her left ear was split in half almost all the way down.

"How could that have happened?" I wondered out loud.

Perhaps she had caught it on a twig while hopping through the woods. Maybe her ear had been injured in a fight with another animal. Of course, I would never know for sure how it happened, but that didn't matter now. The bunny mom had survived the winter and was busily checking out my flowerpots! I watched with anticipation. Would she choose one for a new litter of babies?

April ended and May began with a splash! Rain, rain, and more rain pounded the earth. I had yet to find any new nests in my flowerpots. Then, unexpectedly, on a bright and crisp Sunday morning, my two young nieces made a startling discovery.

Jessica ran into the house at top speed and exclaimed, "We just saw a bunny sitting in the flowerpot by the front door!"

Four-year-old Nicole asked excitedly, "Do you think it could be the bunny mom? Do you think she had more babies?"

"Let's go check it out," I replied as I headed for the front door. Sure enough, there was the bunny mom, sitting calmly on the front porch. "Hello," I greeted her. "I see you found other flowerpots to explore."

The three of us went out to inspect the pots. Carefully moving dirt and fur, we found five newborn bunnies cozy in their nest. Still very young, they had closed eyes and not much fur. Tucked among the bright pink flowers, they snuggled close to each other.

"Well, here we go again," I said with a laugh. Although delighted to see this new little family, I knew the perils we had to face and the job that needed to be done. I explained to my nieces that the babies would be safe for a while, but once they could hop out of the nest they would be in danger of getting lost. It would also be difficult for them to hop back into the rather high flowerpot.

"Will the bunny mom be upset if you check on them every day?" Nicole asked me.

"Not at all," I replied. "Unlike a bird, a rabbit will return to its nest even if people have touched it. This mother rabbit is very comfortable with me. Otherwise, I don't think she would continue to make her nest so close to my house."

Now the watch began. As the torrential rains of May continued, I shielded the nest with an umbrella. At times, I had to cover the umbrella itself with a red slicker to keep it from blowing away in the wind. I knew that the bunny mom had no fear of umbrellas, and she still hopped faithfully into the pot each day to feed her babies.

When the rain subsided, my daughter Catherine and I devised a way to lower the nest by removing half of the dirt in the flowerpot. This would keep the babies safer for a longer time but would still allow the mom to get in and out of the pot easily. We made sure to keep the flowers in the pot to camouflage the nest from possible predators.

I enjoyed gazing out my front door while the bunny mom nursed and cleaned her babies. I had the perfect spot to keep an eye on things and to take some great photographs.

At the end of the third week of our bunny watch, on a very stormy night, we finally decided to bring the baby bunnies into our house. We prepared cages filled with soft hay and made tiny bottles of formula, special milk for baby animals. The bunny family became part of our family now for a brief time. The bunny mom did come to look for her babies, but I think she knew they would be safe with us. I told her once again not to worry.

My children continued the tradition of giving the bunnies flower names. Iris, Lily, and Violet were the three tiny girl bunnies. The boys were Snapdragon and Cracker Jack II who, as the proud and obvious protector of the group, inherited his brother's name! He seemed to be busy plotting his escape from the very beginning.

Over the next four weeks, my daughters and I cared for the bunnies. Emily was the expert when it came to holding each squirmy rabbit as it was fed. Soon the babies learned to lick from a bowl and then began to munch on fresh green clover. Every afternoon, I would drive to a large field and pick baskets of clover to feed the little, but steadily growing, bunnies.

One day, as I was cleaning out and replacing the hay in their cage, I told the boys, "Don't worry. We will let you free soon. Your family is waiting in the yard. I see your mom every day." Just then, Cracker Jack II jumped up and attacked the big gardening glove that I was wearing. "Hey you, tough guy," I said. "It's only a glove! Don't panic." I laughed as he wrestled with my hand. He probably imagined he was fighting off a monster.

The rabbits grew and grew over the next several weeks. Their release back into the wild took place on a perfect July evening. The bunny mom watched closely as we brought out the cages and set her babies free!

We stood and watched them as they circled us in the yard, running and exploring. It made me happy and a little sad too that we had to say good-bye.

Later that evening, I spotted the bunny mom from my kitchen window. She was resting in the twilight with Iris, Violet, and Lily. I suspected that Cracker Jack II and Snapdragon were off playing or investigating their new territory.

Now I found myself waiting again. I knew that rabbits usually have three to four litters a year, so I periodically checked the flowerpots for any new nests.

During the month of August, my daughter Emily and her friend babysat for a group of young girls. They were playing a game of tag in the backyard when all of a sudden I heard screams and saw a lot of commotion! Rushing out to the yard, I pushed my way into the circle of girls. One of them had tripped over a small hole in the ground and unearthed a nest.

"Look, look!" they cried. "Baby mice!"

I looked closely and chuckled. "No," I told them, "they are not mice – they are baby rabbits. You can tell by looking at their ears. I wonder if they belong to the bunny mom."

After everyone had a chance to sneak a peek at the newborn bunnies, I covered the nest with fur and grass and told the girls to be careful not to step on it while they were playing.

As I pondered this new situation, I decided that the bunnies were probably safer here in the lawn than in a flowerpot. At the very least, they would not be able to fall out.

But what dangers would they face here in the middle of the yard? I knew they would have little protection against rain, heat, and other animals. Then I remembered that the gardeners would soon be here to mow the lawn - that could be disastrous! My first decision in helping the bunnies was to cover this area of the lawn with a small table - that would protect the nest from the rain and heat. Would it scare the bunny mom? The answer was no! Later that afternoon I spied her settled right under the little table, nursing her babies. She was fearless!

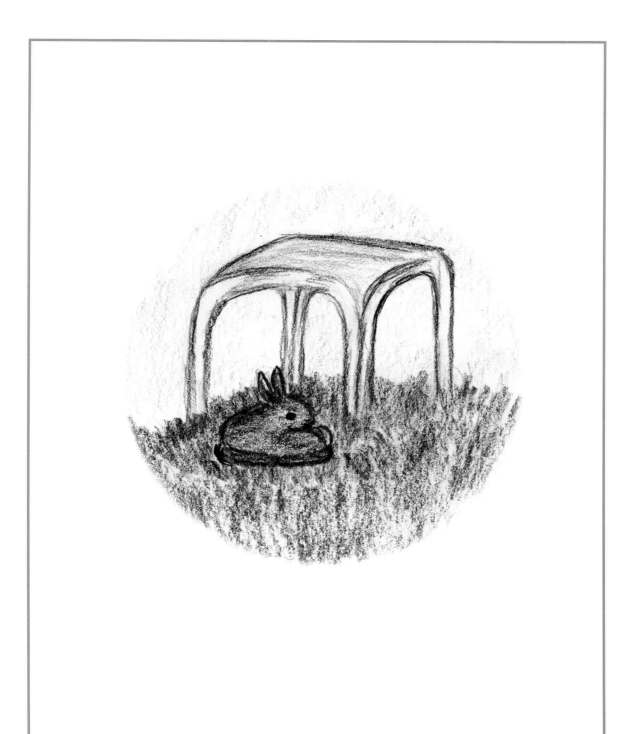

That Friday when our gardeners arrived to mow the lawn, I went out to show them the bunny nest.

"Please be very careful," I said.

"Don't worry," the men replied. "We will mow around the nest."

I thanked them and watched through the kitchen window. I wondered how the baby bunnies felt when the earth rumbled as the mower passed by. The nest was secure for the time being, and I hoped that the bunny mom would continue to be able to care for her babies until they left the nest on their own.

The next week I was waiting outside when the gardeners returned. This time as the mower rumbled by the nest, it scared the bunnies so much that they jumped onto the lawn in a panic! They were still very tiny so they couldn't hop very far. The two gardeners and I scrambled around the yard to scoop them all up. All of a sudden one of the gardeners pointed to a spot right near my feet. There sat the bunny mom! We stared at her in disbelief.

"Let me introduce you to the bunny mom," I said to the men. "She just wants to make sure her babies are all right."

I turned to the bunny mom and explained, "Everyone is fine. I am going to bring your babies to the deck until the men finish mowing. Don't worry."

So I ran to get a small bucket and we put the bunnies inside. Once the mowing was finished, I put the babies back into their nest. I spotted the bunny mom peering out from the woods.

That evening, against a sunset of brilliant reds and oranges, the bunny mom returned to sit calmly under the little table and care for her babies once again.

This new little band of baby bunnies thrived outside and learned to scamper into the woods when they sensed danger. They did not need my assistance any further, so I was content to enjoy watching them. As the summer faded away and the crisp winds of autumn arrived, I saw numerous bunny families living in my backyard. They were the children and grandchildren of the bunny mom. But I never saw the bunny mom that fall after her last litter was big enough to leave their nest in that backyard hole. I feared something might have happened to her or that maybe she had moved to another yard.

Although I did not see the bunny mom on the deck or in the flowerpots, I was surprised one crisp October day to see a gray squirrel busily digging in the largest pot. "What are you doing?" I asked.

When the squirrel was finished and had scurried away, I went out to inspect the pot. Nervously, I pushed the dirt aside. "No babies," I observed with a sigh of relief. I knew squirrels usually make their nests in trees, but things didn't always happen as I expected. There was, instead, a large supply of nuts buried underneath the dirt in the flowerpot. "This pot certainly has many uses!" I exclaimed. I scooped the dirt back over the squirrel's winter food supply.

As winter began again, the face of the world shifted. Snow fell, the hours of light grew shorter, and temperatures dropped.

The bunny mom was gone. For over two years now she'd sat outside my bedroom window almost every evening as the light waned. But now she was not there. In fact, even as the next spring approached, I never saw her. I looked out every day in the hope of spotting her, but it only made me feel sad and lonely when I didn't.

I began to realize that this adventuresome and trusting mother bunny had come to mean a great deal to me. We shared a bond of friendship and caring. I had become a part of her family and she was part of mine. What would I do without her?

Throughout the spring, many neighborly bunnies hopped about and munched clover in my backyard, but there was still no sign of the bunny mom. I figured she was injured or lost to the cold of winter. My heart ached for her but I also knew that most rabbits only live for one to two years in the wild.

I was determined to keep my eye on her children, however. Although it might seem strange to think of wild animals as pets, that is how I felt about all these bunnies. Through the years, my children insisted on having pets in our home. So we had an assortment of animals, including fish, hamsters, a guinea pig, rabbits, a lizard, a chinchilla, two dogs, and even a horse, which of course we kept in a barn!

When I thought back on how the Flowerpot Bunnies adventure began, I guess it was no surprise that my daughter Emily knew I would care about the baby bunnies and want to help them. She had a heart of gold, especially when it came to animals. I felt from the beginning that I could not let her down.

Just when we all thought the bunny mom would never return, one bright June morning I looked out my front door and there she was, sitting bold as you please on my front porch! The bunny mom turned to look at me.

"Welcome back, dear friend," I whispered to her. "I thought you were gone forever." I opened the door and sat on the front step to watch her. I smiled as I wondered what new adventures she had planned for my family and me.

Meet Tucker and Learn About Domestic Rabbits!

Tucker

Tucker is an eighteen-month-old dwarf rabbit who weighs about five pounds. He is very friendly and loves to be petted. He enjoys hopping around and playing in his cage, but also has fun just relaxing in his soft chair. When he was young, his favorite place to hang out was his little wooden house. Tucker eats Timothy hay, rabbit pellets, and of course, carrots. He is particularly fond of meeting children who have read The Flowerpot Bunnies!

Domestic Rabbits

Unlike wild rabbits, domestic rabbits are raised to be pets. There are many different breeds of exotic rabbits and they are bred all over the world. Rabbits are excellent pets for many families. They are clean, quiet, and love to play and cuddle. They even enjoy playing with toys.

Rabbits range in weight from two to sixteen pounds, depending on their breed. They can be litter-trained just like kittens. Pet rabbits eat prepared pellets, different types of hay and fresh vegetables. They are generally healthy and don't require vaccinations, but should be followed by a veterinarian.

Some domestic rabbits have pointed ears that stand up straight, while lop breeds have floppy ears that hang down. All rabbits have excellent hearing and vision! Above is a picture of Chelsea, a lop-eared bunny.

Meet the
REAL
Flowerpot Bunnies!

Snapdragon

The Bunny Mom

Cracker Jack II

Iris, Violet and Lily

Nest in the Lawn

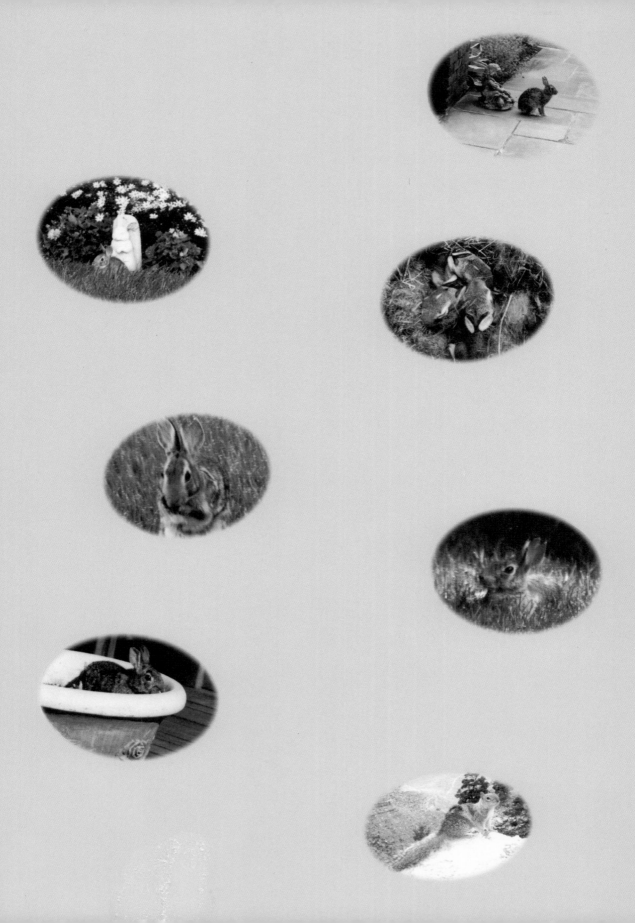